Tiny Toes

Donna Jakob

ILLUSTRATED BY MIREILLE LEVERT

HYPERION BOOKS FOR CHILDREN
NEW YORK

T iny toes
peek out from
under the bedcovers.

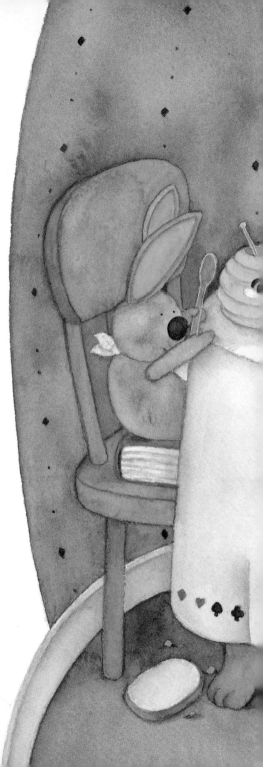

C rumbly toes
waltz around
the breakfast table.

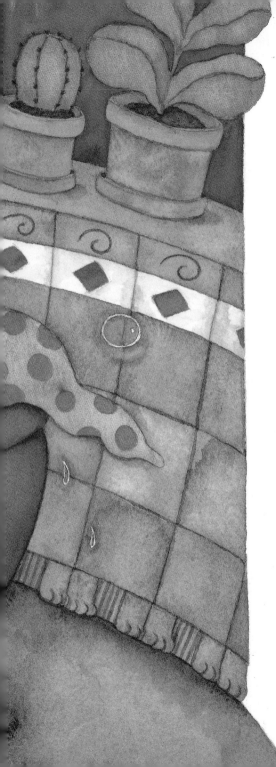

B̲ubbly toes
soak in a
warm tub.

D irty toes
squish through
muddy spring puddles.

Kicky toes
scatter dandelions
into the breeze.

Wiggly toes
poke through the straps
of new sandals.

Splashy toes
paddle
in the pool.

Dressy toes
prance
in patent leather.

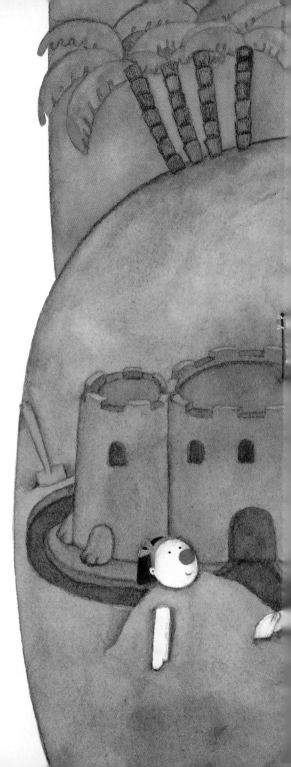

Sandy toes
stomp on
castles and moats.

Sweaty toes
hide inside socks
worn to the park.

Skippy toes
find pebbles
hidden in the grass.

Jumpy toes
leap in piles
of autumn leaves.

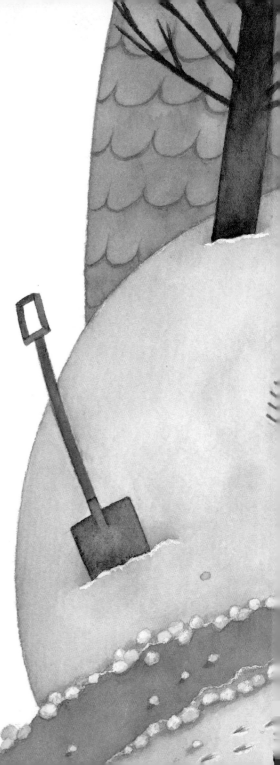

Frosty toes
plow through drifts
of winter snow.

Cozy toes
warm
by an evening fire.

Sleepy toes
snuggle in
woolly pajamas.

For
Emma and Hannah,
with love
– D.J.

For
my sister
and her three little girls
– M.L.

Text © 1995 by Donna Jakob.
Illustrations © 1995 by Mireille Levert.
All rights reserved.
Printed in Hong Kong.
For information address Hyperion Books for Children,
114 Fifth Avenue, New York, New York 10011.
FIRST EDITION
1   3   5   7   9   10   8   6   4   2
Library of Congress Cataloging-in-Publication Data
Jakob, Donna.
Tiny toes/by Donna Jakob; illustrated by Mireille Levert —
1st ed.
p.   cm.
Summary: Describes children, focusing on their toes, as they
dance, splash, wiggle, stomp, and leap their way through a variety
of activities.
ISBN 0-7868-0013-5 (trade) — ISBN 0-7868-2009-8 (lib. bdg.)
[1. Toes — Fiction.   2. Play — Fiction.]   I. Levert, Mireille, ill.
II. Title.
PZ7.J153554Ti   1995
[E] — dc20   93-40846   CIP   AC

The artwork for each picture is prepared using watercolor.
The book is set in 27-point Post Antiqua.